With ♡;
Happiness!

[signature] 2013

That's Happiness © 2012
A Virtue Soup Enterprises Production

Author - Cisco Robbins Davis
Illustrations - Adrianne Davis
Cover Photo - Claire Pullinger
Publishing Services - Joe Dully

ISBN-978-0-9858152-0-2
First Edition

To order additional copies or the audio version of this book, please visit our website at

www.ThatsHappiness.com

Paper used for the pages of this book are Forest Stewardship Counsel Certified

Printed in the USA

To Cidney, my true love and my inspiration.

THAT'S HAPPINESS

AN ADVENTURE IN BUDDHISM
FOR CHILDREN OF ALL AGES

by Cisco Davis

Little did Mr. Brambles know when he woke up that morning, what a special day it was going to be. Mr. Brambles was a very lucky bunny. He had soft white fur with big brown spots, and fuzzy brown ears that flipped and flopped when he ran. His eyes sparkled when he smiled, which was almost all the time.

He lived with his favorite person in the whole world, Eleanor. She had found Mr. Brambles while walking in the woods on a grey and rainy day. Mr. Brambles, just a baby bunny then, had ventured deep into the blackberry bush to get the few remaining berries of the season. As he leaned *way* in to get the *very* last blackberry, the thorns on the vine caught his fur. The more he tugged to get free, the more stuck he became. That's when Eleanor passed him on the path. She spotted something in the bushes and bent down to get a closer look.

"Oh you dear little bunny," she exclaimed, "don't be afraid. I'll get you out of there." So Mr. Brambles held very still and let Eleanor untangle his shivering little body. From that day forward they were best of friends and, as you may have guessed, that's how Mr. Brambles got his name.

CHAPTER ONE

Mr. Brambles went home that day with Eleanor. A warm fire burned in the big rock fireplace, and as Mr. Brambles hopped through the doorway, the smell of fresh baked bread and cinnamon filled his nose. The house was small, but very cheerful. The floors were made of brick, and the walls were painted yellow. Pots of bright red geraniums were placed in front of the windows, and a big clock that looked like the moon hung on the wall, ticking and tocking happily.

Eleanor made Mr. Brambles his own little bed, right next to hers. He was home.

It wasn't long before Mr. Brambles felt like he had lived in this wonderful house all his life. His favorite place to be was in Eleanor's lap as she nodded off to sleep in her big stuffed chair in front of the fireplace. The chair was a bit tattered and, if you looked closely, you could see many places where Eleanor had taken her needle and thread and stitched up small tears and holes. Still, to Mr. Brambles, it was the most wonderful place a little bunny could ever be.

Everything in the house was small except the kitchen. In the center was a large oven surrounded by shelves of bright colored mixing bowls and muffin tins. Shiny pans dangled from hooks on the ceiling, which didn't really matter, because Eleanor wasn't very tall so she never banged her head. Eleanor had learned to bake from her grandmother, who had learned all of her special secret recipes from her grandmother. All the town knew of Eleanor's delicious homemade creations.

CHAPTER TWO

Every morning when Mr. Brambles woke up, he knew Eleanor was busy baking before he even opened his eyes. He could hear her humming softly, which she always did when she baked. She once told Mr. Brambles that was part of her secret and it just seemed to make things taste better. Eleanor made muffins nearly every morning, and Mr. Brambles' nose told him they were almost ready. He yawned, stretched, and hopped out of his little bed.

"Well, good morning, sleepy head," said Eleanor. "I'm ready to go do my deliveries. Are you coming along?" She knew the answer and didn't really have to ask. Mr. Brambles loved deliveries. He turned and raced to the cupboard where Eleanor kept his special blanket, almost crashing into the cupboard door as he slid to a stop. He knew the routine well. She would wrap him up snugly in his blanket and put him in the little box she'd fastened to the handle bars of her bicycle, just for him. With her basket of muffins safely strapped to the back of the bike, they would head off together through the brisk morning fog.

Mr. Brambles loved to pretend he was the brave skipper of a sailing ship. As Eleanor pedaled along the path, he imagined himself navigating a great ocean. Ears flapping, he loved the breeze in his face and the smell of wet leaves and smoke from the chimneys of the houses they passed on their way.

Today was Sunday and that meant their first stop was the Buddhist Temple. Every week Eleanor delivered fresh muffins for the people attending the Temple to enjoy after the early morning service. As they approached, Mr. Brambles felt a familiar excitement. Eleanor parked the bike by the back door, tucked Mr. Brambles in her big apron pocket, and quietly stepped inside with her basket of muffins.

The large reception room was paneled with dark wood. There was soft lighting, and long tables were filled with fruit, cookies and lines of tea cups. Eleanor helped the woman with the warm smile and rosy cheeks who greeted them, arrange the muffins.

The woman's name was Molly. She was the caretaker for the Temple and an old school friend of Eleanor's. They were a little early today so Molly asked Eleanor to join her for a cup of tea. They loved to spend time together sharing memories of their childhood.

Mr. Brambles peeked out over the edge of Eleanor's apron pocket when he smelled the cookie on the napkin in her lap. He leaned out as far as he could stretch for a nibble and *boom*, tumbled head first onto the floor. Eleanor was so busy chatting, she didn't even notice he was gone.

"Oh boy," he thought, "an adventure. Mr. Brambles the Great Explorer!" He hopped under a table, so he could get a clear view of the room. At the far end was a set of huge wooden doors. He decided he had better have a closer look and silently hopped over. One of the doors was cracked open just wide enough for him to peek inside. He leaned in and froze in his tracks. He had never seen anything like this before!

CHAPTER THREE

The large room was glowing with candlelight. The high ceiling was round with carved wooden beams that met in the middle like the spokes of a wheel. Beautiful tapestries with every color of the rainbow hung on the walls from red and gold ribbons. Everywhere were bunches of flowers, crystal bowls and small statues of elephants, deer and other magical creatures. Immediately a peaceful feeling came over Mr. Brambles. It felt like he had walked into a dream.

In the front of the room was a small platform where a woman sat cross legged on a velvet cushion. Behind her were three grand golden statues of what looked like people from some faraway place. The loving smile on the face of the statue in the middle caught Mr. Brambles' eye. He smiled back.

Rows of benches filled with people faced the woman on the velvet cushion. She was not a very large woman, but she had the attention of everyone in the room. She spoke with a calm, soothing voice and her eyes sparkled as she talked. She had very short grey hair and smiling green eyes. She wore gold and crimson robes and a pair of glasses that rested on the end of her nose.

"Pssssst…Pssssst…"

Mr. Brambles jumped, and looked around to see a very small orange kitty smiling at him from behind one of the benches. Mr. Brambles quietly hopped over to her.

"Hi," she said, "what are you doing here?"

"I'm not really sure," Mr. Brambles replied. "I kind of found my way by accident. What about you?" he asked.

"I live here," she told him. "My name is Squirt."

"I like that name," he said. "I'm Mr. Brambles."

"Well it's awfully nice to make your acquaintance, Mr. Brambles," she smiled.

The woman at the front of the room was just finishing her talk. "So…If we want to find true happiness," she said, "something we can practice each day is Patience. Until we meet again next week, try to be a little more patient and just see what happens. Let everything you think, say and do, be for the benefit of all."

She put the palms of her hands together in front of her heart and bowed to the audience. The people on the benches did the same and bowed back to her.

"Gosh," said Mr. Brambles, "I'd better find my way back. Goodbye, Squirt."

"Come back to visit again soon," Squirt answered, as he disappeared.

Somehow Mr. Brambles managed to weave silently in between the legs of the people in the crowd as they chatted happily and made their way to the reception room. Eleanor had not even noticed that Mr. Brambles was missing, so imagine her surprise when he leaped up into her arms and snuggled back down into her apron pocket.

CHAPTER FOUR
~ PATIENCE ~

That night Mr. Brambles curled up in Eleanor's lap in their favorite chair in front of the fire. He couldn't stop thinking about his wonder filled day. He thought about Squirt, his new friend, and the soothing voice of the woman on the velvet cushion. What did she mean when she said they should practice patience?

He knew what he had to do. He had to talk to his friend Hillary, the hawk.

The next morning Mr. Brambles couldn't wait to get going. Eleanor was busy baking and humming. She smiled and said, "Good morning," and bent down to kiss him softly on the head. He scampered out the door and shivered when he felt the chill of the morning air. Winter had come and the forest was a shimmering white. He hopped along the path, watching the sky for his friend. Hillary was up early, too, soaring high above the tops of the trees now dusted with snow. She spotted Mr. Brambles far below and flew down to greet him.

His heart jumped. He was so happy to see her as she gracefully landed on the path beside him.

"Hello, old friend," said Hillary.

"Hi, Hillary," he grinned.

The sun peeked up over the mountain and the morning light danced and glimmered on the snow. "What brings you out so early on this beautiful day?" she asked.

"I was looking for you," he replied. "I know you spend each day soaring high above the forest. You can see everything below. Your view of the world has brought you great wisdom. I want to know what it means to have patience. Can you help me?"

Hillary ruffled her feathers and tilted her head from side to side. She was a magnificent creature. More than twice the size of a little bunny, she had broad powerful wings and strong feathered legs. Her proud beak shone yellow like the sun and her sharp black eyes were deep and knowing.

"To be patient," she said, "is to understand that everything happens in its own time. When old man Turtle is blocking your path, and you can't get by to hurry on your way, that's the time you must remember patience. If you get mad, it won't make him

go any faster. He's a turtle! You'll probably just hurt his feelings and upset yourself. The lesson is that no matter what is happening around you, you have a choice about how you are going to feel."

Hillary continued, "It's like that afternoon last spring when we planned a picnic with Adrianne, the bear. Do you remember? She got so distracted when she passed by the bee family's hive and smelled the honey, she was late to meet us and we all had to wait. We happily accepted the delay, and just made a joke about our good friend, the hungry bear. Then we had a lovely time picking flowers until she caught up with us. We were patient, and we felt better inside. When we truly learn the gift of patience, we will find inner peace. When we have inner peace, we can be happy all the time. The best part is when we are happy, we make others happy, too. I think that's what life is all about."

"Wow," said Mr. Brambles, "I never saw it that way before. Thank you, Hillary, that really helped."

"Oh, you are welcome, my friend. Must be on my way now. I hope to see you again very soon. Stay warm." And with that, off she flew. Mr. Brambles watched until the giant bird was just a small speck in the sky.

CHAPTER FIVE

Mr. Brambles couldn't wait until next Sunday. Through the week Eleanor baked her muffins and, with Mr. Brambles bundled up in his special box on the handle bars, she made her deliveries around the town. First to the café where they sometimes stopped for hot chocolate to get warm, then to the little store where Mrs. Spencer always gave Mr. Brambles a carrot wrapped up in a tiny bow. Eleanor's muffins didn't last long on Mrs. Spencer's shelves, so they sometimes returned with more before the end of the week. They delivered to the kindergarten, the hospital and the fire station where Eleanor donated her muffins to the brave firefighters. What a wonderful full life for a bunny.

On Sunday morning Eleanor finished baking her muffins and looked around to find Mr. Brambles already sitting, waiting *patiently*, of course, by the door. With muffins and bunny securely on board, Eleanor pedaled carefully down the snowy path.

As they approached the Temple, Mr. Brambles could see Squirt peeking out the window. She meowed, and he smiled up at her.

Molly opened the door and Eleanor, with Mr. Brambles tucked in her apron pocket, stepped into the toasty room.

"Good morning," Molly greeted her old friend, "it's so nice to see you again. You're very early today."

"Well, I didn't have to wait for my sleepy head little bunny today," Eleanor smiled. "He was up even before the rooster this morning." She gave Mr. Brambles a wink.

They busily arranged the muffins on the long tables. "Would you like to sit in on the service today?" Molly asked Eleanor. "It always seems to brighten my day when I do."

"Am I dressed all right?" asked Eleanor.

"That's the beautiful thing about the Buddhists," Molly smiled warmly, "everyone is welcome and how you dress is always just perfect."

Eleanor nodded. They quietly opened the large wooden doors and stepped into the room. Molly and Eleanor found a seat on a bench and Mr. Brambles made himself comfortable on Eleanor's lap. He heard purring and looked over to see his new friend, Squirt. She hopped up on Molly's lap and greeted Mr. Brambles.

In the front of the room, the woman with the calm voice sat on her cushion.

"I'm sure you all practiced patience last week," she said with a smile, "and you don't seem to be any worse for wear. Today I want to talk about a simple thing called Kindness. Close your eyes a moment. What does it mean to you to be kind?" Everyone sat quietly until she spoke again.

"You probably thought about saying or doing something nice for a friend. Yes, you got it, kindness is that. But, it is so much more. Kindness is not just about what you do, it is about what you say and what you think. It's not just being kind to your family and friends, it is also about being kind to yourself and every other living being. Your job this week is to try to be kind to everyone, with every thought, word and deed. Good luck. I know you can do it."

CHAPTER SIX
~ KINDNESS ~

Eleanor and Mr. Brambles headed for home. Icicles dangled from the trees, and the forest looked like a shimmering white wonderland. As they came around the corner, and their house came into view, they could see someone knocking at their door. Mr. Brambles would know that long fluffy red tail anywhere. It was his friend Sam, the fox.

Sam and Mr. Brambles had played together since they were small. Mr. Brambles thought Sam was the most handsome animal in the forest. His beautiful red coat had streaks of brown and black, giving him an interesting, distinguished look. His sharp black eyes shone like jewels.

"Well howdy, Mr. B.," said Sam. "How's my good bunny buddy?"

"I'm doing just great," replied Mr. Brambles. "I'm happy to see you."

"A few of us are getting together in the meadow to build a snowman. Want to come along?" asked Sam.

"You bet," said Mr. Brambles, and off they went.

When they got to the clearing, Mr. Brambles could see animals of all shapes and sizes playing in the snow. In the center of the meadow a raccoon, a couple of squirrels, a deer, an elk, a bear and a chipmunk were busily building a giant snowman. Other animals slipped and slid on a frozen pond. An otter and a young beaver raced each other down a snowy hill, sliding on their bellies.

Sam and Mr. Brambles joined the snowman builders. A deer had made a hat out of leaves. She set the hat on top of the elk's great antlers, and he carefully placed it on the snowman's head.

Mr. Brambles set out to find the perfect nose for the snowman. He headed toward the edge of the meadow and spotted a skunk and a porcupine, off by themselves, sitting on a fallen tree.

"Hello there," he said. As he approached them he could see they looked sad. "Why are you sitting over here by yourselves?" he asked. "Why don't you come and join the fun?"

"I smell funny," said the skunk.

"And I keep poking the other animals with my sharp quills," the porcupine added. "We don't feel like we fit in."

Mr. Brambles picked up a large pinecone he spotted on the ground and turned back to the skunk and the porcupine. "Let me go deliver this nose for the snowman, and then you are invited to come back to my house with me. There is no better cure for being a little sad, than a cup of Eleanor's hot apple cider and one of her frosted ginger cookies."

The three new friends spent the day playing together and had a most wonderful time. When Mr. Brambles finally came in, cold and tired, he was happy to see Eleanor already reading in front of the fire. He jumped up onto her lap and curled up into a ball while she gently stroked his ears.

"Do you know what a special little bunny you are?" Eleanor smiled warmly. "You didn't judge the skunk and porcupine for their smell or their prickliness. You were loving and thoughtful and most of all, a good friend. When the wise woman at the Temple spoke to us about kindness this morning, I think that treating others the way you treated your friends today, is what she was talking about."

A very tired little Mr. Brambles was soon fast asleep in Eleanor's lap.

CHAPTER SEVEN

Spring had come to the little village where Eleanor and Mr. Brambles lived. The last of the snow finally melted and flowers of every color popped up all around them. They had spent Sunday mornings at the Temple, soaking in the beautiful words and thoughts of the loving woman on the velvet cushion. Today she was talking about Contentment.

"That's an awfully big word," thought Mr. Brambles, "contentment, hmm." He hopped down and went off to join Squirt, who was playing quietly at the back of the room.

From the corner they heard a whisper. "Hey, over here," came a small voice. They looked up to see a little grey mouse smiling back at them. She was out of breath. She motioned them over to the corner. It was Natalie, the Temple mouse.

"Hi, Natalie," Squirt said to her friend. "I'd like you to meet Mr. Brambles."

"Good to meet you, Mr. Brambles," Natalie replied. "Now follow me, you two. I have something I want to show you."

Squirt and Natalie weren't always friends. When Squirt first moved in with Molly, as the Temple caretaker's kitty, she would chase Natalie and try to pounce on the little mouse. Natalie was always too quick and she thought it was funny. Soon it became a game of hide and seek and before long they were chasing each other and crashing into benches and laughing until they were exhausted.

Natalie drew Squirt and Mr. Brambles closer. "I have found a secret passage way!" she whispered excitedly. "I don't know where it leads."

"Well, let's find out," said Mr. Brambles the Adventurer.

"Are you sure?" Squirt asked. "What if there's danger?"

"We'll be careful," the little mouse replied. "We just need to make sure we can find our way back."

The three explorers set off with Natalie in the lead. She disappeared behind a big oak bookcase in the corner of the room. The other two followed cautiously.

They realized that the bookcase was covering a small hole in the wall. Natalie popped through the hole and motioned to her friends to follow. Squirt went first and Mr. Brambles' heart pounded as he hopped through the opening. A window high above gave enough light for them to see that behind the wall was an abandoned staircase. For some reason it had been boarded up, and from the thick dust and cobwebs all around, it looked like it had been sealed up a long, long time ago.

Silently, Natalie, Squirt and Mr. Brambles crept down the staircase. When Natalie stepped on a creaky stair, the eerie noise made Mr. Brambles jump. He tried not to look scared. Down, down, down they went. Step by step, slowly and carefully. Finally, they reached the bottom. Before them was an old wooden door with a big brass knob. The knob was too high to reach.

"That's O.K.," Squirt whispered. "Let's just head back."

Natalie was scratching her head. "Hmm," she said thoughtfully, "we need a plan. We can't turn back now… I've got it!"

She told Squirt to climb up on Mr. Brambles' shoulders. Then she stood back and took a run at them and scrambled up to the top of Squirt's head. Squirt gave her a little boost and she grabbed the brass knob.

It creaked loudly as it turned and the door swung open. The three tried to be quiet and not to start laughing as they tumbled onto the floor. Arm in arm, the brave explorers tip-toed into the dark room. They looked up and everybody froze. Ten pairs of tiny red eyes were staring back at them.

The hair on Mr. Brambles' back stood straight up. Squirt jumped behind him and peeked around slowly.

"Welcome," came a voice from behind one of the pairs of red eyes. "We are the spider family. We are so glad you're here. We rarely get visitors." All the little spiders giggled as the three guests breathed one big sigh of relief.

"This was once a secret chamber, long, long ago," the elder spider continued. "It held treasure maps and magic potions. It held secrets, which if told, were said to bring happiness." The old spider paused and smiled at his awestruck audience.

"So what happened?" Natalie asked.

"Well," said the spider as he sat back on six of his black hairy legs, "people found the treasure, used the magic potions and learned the secrets. At first they were happy, or at least thought they were. After a while, though, the excitement about these things just kind of wore off. People looked around and realized they had been happier with the lives, friends, and things they had before they had discovered this room. Everyone decided to work together and seal off the staircase and to get back to their homes and their families."

CHAPTER EIGHT
~ CONTENTMENT ~

In the big room above the secret chamber, Eleanor sat on the bench deep in thought. The wise woman at the front of the room had explained that you will find contentment when you want what you have, and you have what you want. If you are trying to find happiness, look again, you may already have it. She had asked the group to imagine themselves living in huge mansions with beautiful furniture, and servants tending to their every need. To see themselves decorated in jewels, driving fast expensive cars, and eating rich exotic foods.

Eleanor pondered it a bit, enjoying the dreamy excitement of it all. "The truth is, though," she thought to herself, "I love my cozy little house and my tattered old chair. I'm warm and happy there. And as for a fancy car, I get around just fine on my bicycle. Besides, it's all set up for my best little pal, Mr. Brambles, to ride up in front where he can see the world. Wait a minute!" she gasped. "Where is Mr. Brambles?"

Just then, around the corner of the big oak bookcase, scrambled Natalie, Squirt and Mr. Brambles. They were panting from the excitement of their adventure and the long climb back up the abandoned stairway. Mr. Brambles did a nose dive deep into the warmth and safety of Eleanor's apron. He had had enough adventure for one day. He was now quite sure he was just where he wanted to be.

CHAPTER NINE

At the Temple the following Sunday, Mr. Brambles stayed close to Eleanor. When she found her seat on one of the benches, he sat right next to her.

At the end of each row of benches were baskets of white candles. The people found their seats, took a candle and passed them along. When everyone else was seated, the small woman in the gold and crimson robes entered the room. She carried a lighted candle that glowed brightly as she began to speak.

"Imagine," she said in her calm, soothing way. "Imagine the flame from this candle I hold is the light that burns inside my heart. It burns with love, compassion and understanding. It burns with joy and hope. It is a part of me."

She then walked over to the first person sitting in the first row. She bent down and lit his candle with hers. He leaned over and lit the candle of the person next to him, and then she lit the candle of the person next to her with her candle. Mr. Brambles watched with amazement as one by one each candle was lit and the light was passed along.

He was ready when it was his turn, and he lit the candle of Squirt, who had jumped up next to him. When everyone in the room was finally holding a lighted candle, the smiling woman in the front took her seat on her cushion. The candlelight danced on the golden statues behind her and the whole room glowed like a giant birthday cake.

"Every light in this room," she said softly, "came from the same flame. Inside each of us burns a similar flame. It is the true voice within us. It is the part of our nature that desires to be kind, generous and loving to one another. By this flame that burns inside us, we are all connected to each other. We are all singing one song."

"This week, try concentrating on living your life with Consideration for Others. Start with showing love to yourself and remember we are all connected. Show all others the same kind of love and care that you would have them show to you. When we are considerate of others, it brings them joy, which then brings us deep inner happiness."

CHAPTER TEN
~ Consideration for Others ~

After the service, Molly invited Eleanor and Mr. Brambles to stay for refreshments with the others. She cut a muffin in two, and put it on a plate for Mr. Brambles and Squirt to share. Mr. Brambles was hungry and quickly grabbed the biggest piece. Suddenly he stopped himself and turned the plate so Squirt could reach the big half.

"Some things feel better than a full tummy," he thought to himself.

Eleanor had been watching dark clouds gathering outside the Temple window and decided it was time for them to be on their way home. As they passed the big meadow, Mr. Brambles could see some of his friends playing near the pond. Mr. Brambles looked up at Eleanor. She nodded. "Yes, go have fun with your friends," she said, "just watch the sky. You don't want to get caught in the storm."

Off he went, so excited to see his pals. Sam, the fox, was there skipping stones across the pond with Adrianne, the bear. Mother Hen was there taking her new baby chick, Melly, on her first outing. There were squirrels, chipmunks, deer and elk. Mr. Brambles smiled to see that even the skunk and porcupine had joined the fun. Hillary, the hawk, sat on the branch of a tree and waved her great wing at Mr. Brambles.

Next to her sat Jule, the old Great Horned owl. Jule was getting on in years and had a little trouble seeing so well.

"That's my friend, Mr. Brambles," Hillary told her. Jule looked down to see and almost lost her balance. Hillary steadied her and scooted her closer.

"You are such a dear to watch out for me," said the proud old owl.

"We all have different gifts to share," the great hawk said warmly, "I'm happy to help."

Mr. Brambles hopped over to join Sam and Adrianne by the water.

"Howdy, Mr. B.," grinned Sam. "Good to see you, old buddy."

Adrianne smiled, waved her large paw, and went back to skipping rocks.

"Hey be careful, you almost winged me," came a voice from the water. Out in the pond Mr. Brambles could see a duck paddling through the water lilies.

"That's The Duck," said Sam. "He's a regular here."

"What's his name?" asked Mr. Brambles.

"For as long as I've known him, I've never heard any other name. Everyone has always just called him, 'The Duck'. I'll introduce you when he gets back to shore."

A raindrop hit Mr. Brambles on the nose. He looked out at the pond and realized it had started raining. First small, then larger drops rippled on the water. A gust of wind blew cold against their backs and suddenly they heard a screech. It was Mother Hen. Her little chick, Melly, had been blown into the pond. Lightning flashed and the thunder made a loud clap. Everyone jumped.

The wind blew harder and Melly was blown further and further from the shore. "Help, someone, help!" cried Mother Hen.

The Duck paddled furiously over to the frightened little chicken. He disappeared under the water and came up seconds later with the chick on his back. There was more lightning and the thunder roared. The Duck fought the rising waves and finally delivered Melly, a shaking little ball of wet feathers, back to shore.

Mother Hen gathered her up and held her close.

"You risked your life to save my chick," said Mother Hen gratefully. "You are so kind."

"I'm sure you'd have done the same for me if you had a chance," replied The Duck. "We all have to look out for each other."

"Thank The Duck," Mother Hen said to little Melly.

Melly said, "Peep!" and he knew what she meant.

Drenched, the whole group headed for home. The storm had passed and the sun peeked out as Mr. Brambles made his way down the path. When he reached his house, the door opened and there was Eleanor carefully setting a spider out on the step.

"Wow, that was close!" Mr. Brambles heard the spider say. "I was stuck in the sink and this really nice lady was about to turn on the water when, thank goodness, she noticed me. I thought I was a goner, but she just gently slid me into a cup and brought me outside."

"I'm so glad she saw you," said Mr. Brambles, "that's Eleanor. She is very kind. My name is Mr. Brambles."

"I'm Dudie," the spider answered. "Hey, you're the bunny who visited my cousins down in the secret chamber. They enjoyed the company. I'll tell them, 'Hello' for you."

Dudie headed off down the path, grateful for Eleanor's big heart.

"Goodbye and be careful!" Mr. Brambles waved and went inside to tell Eleanor all about his exciting day.

CHAPTER ELEVEN

The following week Eleanor pedaled her trusty bike to the Temple through the spring morning air with Mr. Brambles at the helm. The smell of warm muffins coming from the basket and the sun in his face, Mr. Brambles the Brave Skipper of the great sailing ship, felt as happy as he could ever remember feeling. He helped Molly and Eleanor put refreshments out on the long tables and entered the great hall quietly with them when everything was perfect.

The wise woman in the front smiled at them as they found their seats among the others on one of the benches.

"I am happy to see all of you," she said, eyes twinkling. "Today

I want to talk to you about Faith. Faith is believing in something you can't see."

"Believing in something I can't see?" thought Mr. Brambles. "But if I can't see it, how do I know there is something there?"

He had learned a lot from the small wise woman with the short grey hair. He didn't always understand at first what she meant, but eventually it made sense to him. He had found that living by following his heart made him happy and the others around him seemed happier, too. He decided to keep his eyes open for something he couldn't see, and jumped down to go find Squirt and Natalie, who were always lots of fun.

CHAPTER TWELVE
~ Faith ~

The warm days of summer passed lazily. Mr. Brambles and his friends played in the meadow almost every day until they finally exhausted themselves and found their way home at supper time. He loved finding ways to practice kindness and consideration for his friends and the people in the village. It made him feel good, and he thought it made them feel good, too.

On Sundays he looked forward to going to the Temple. He liked having something he and Eleanor did together, and they both always felt so warm inside after listening to the gentle woman's calm soothing voice. One Sunday morning Eleanor stayed to help Molly clean up after everyone had gone and the two got to talking about old times.

"This could take a while," thought Mr. Brambles. He decided to go find Squirt and Natalie and headed for the great hall. He felt small all alone in the big room. He was scouting for his pals between the rows of benches, when someone touched him on the shoulder. He froze and slowly turned around. It was the wise woman in the gold and crimson robes.

"Hello, dear one," she said softly, "I'm glad to finally meet you. I understand you are a very kind and thoughtful little bunny."

Mr. Brambles just smiled. He couldn't think of a thing to say. Then it came to him. Many times since the day she had talked about faith, Mr. Brambles had thought and wondered about what she meant. He had to ask.

"Uh, I don't understand what faith is," he said shyly.

She sat down on the floor next to him, looked into his eyes, and answered, "Buddha says faith is like legs, supreme legs with which you run toward happiness. Faith is a gift that allows us to believe in things we can't see. Faith starts in your heart. It is something that you feel, not something that you think."

"Mr. Brambles," she went on, "have you ever seen a flock of wild geese flying across the sky?"

He nodded yes.

"Every year they gather together and leave their home when the weather turns cold. They fly far, far away to spend the winter where they will be comfortable and warm. When spring comes, they gather again and head back home. How do they know where they are going? How do they know they'll find their way back home?"

"They have faith?" asked Mr. Brambles.

"Yes, young one," she said, "they have faith."

"Faith gives you special energy to live in a positive way. It is as if there is a lighted path and if you trust that that path will get you where you need to be, you will find your way. I have seen you listening carefully to my teachings over the past few months. You have learned about Patience, Kindness, Contentment and Consideration for Others. When we steer our lives, as best we can toward living these things for the benefit of all, we find true happiness. We have fewer problems and more fun. By just changing our minds, we help ourselves and help others."

The kind woman bent down and gave Mr. Brambles a soft kiss on the top of his head. She bowed and smiled at him, her green eyes sparkling. He bowed his head respectfully and scampered back to find Eleanor.

CHAPTER THIRTEEN
~ It Matters ~

That evening in front of the glowing fire, together in the big old chair, Eleanor and Mr. Brambles sat quietly. Both deep in thought about the events of the day, they were sure they could have faith in one thing, their love for each other.

"Mr. Brambles," Eleanor said, "you are growing up to be an amazing young bunny. I watch how you treat others. You try never to cause fear, suffering or pain to any other living creature. You have learned to be happy with who you are, where you are and what you have, no matter what else is happening."

"Imagine," she said, "that the pond where you skip rocks is very still and calm. When you throw a pebble into the water, the ripples seem to go on endlessly. Well, you are like that pebble. All of your acts of loving kindness go out and affect those around you, who then affect those around them. You are spreading joy and loving kindness further than you can know or see."

Mr. Brambles yawned sleepily. Eleanor took him gently from her lap and tucked him into his little bed. "The most important thing," she whispered, "is that you can make a big difference that benefits all living beings, even if you are just one little bunny. Good night, Mr. Brambles."

The End

The Real Mr. Brambles

THAT'S HAPPINESS is inspired by a true story. The real Mr. Brambles had been abandoned and was found tangled in a berry bush by Mel Watson and Jen Todd of Whidbey Island, Washington. They took him home where he now lives with a wonderful family of bunnies that they have rescued over the years.

Mel and Jen are members of a Buddhist Temple in Seattle. Once on a short visit to the Temple, Mr. Brambles was allowed to go along. Of course, it's no surprise, he had fun and made a lot of new friends.

From left to right, a felt bunny made by someone at
the Temple, Mr. Brambles' girlfriend, Miss Sniffles
June Dalton, and Mr. Brambles.